for Tim and Emily
with love
~ P.L.

for Aaron
~ P.I.

LITTLE TIGER PRESS LTD,
an imprint of the Little Tiger Group
1 Coda Studios, 189 Munster Road, London SW6 6AW
www.littletiger.co.uk

First published in Great Britain 2000
This edition published 2005

Printed in China • LTP/2900/2777/0319
4 6 8 10 9 7 5

I'll Always Love You

Paeony Lewis

Penny Ives

LITTLE TIGER

LONDON

One morning Alex woke early
and ran downstairs to the kitchen.
"I'll make Mum some toast and
honey for breakfast," he said.
"She'll like that."

Alex reached for the honey bowl and . . .

CRASH!

. . . his mum's favourite bowl was now nine pieces of sticky china.

Alex hadn't *meant* to break it. What would she say?

Alex's mum was doing her morning exercises.
"Hello, Alex," she said. "Did I hear something break?"
"Mum, will you only love me if I'm good?" asked Alex.

"I'll always love you," said his mum, and she smiled.

"Even when I've done something that *isn't* good?" asked Alex.

"I'll still love you," said his mum. "Honest."

"What if I have a pillow fight with Joey Bear and all the feathers burst out? Will you still love me?"
"I'll always love you. Though you must pick up all the feathers."

"What if I spill my new pots of paint on Baby
Pog and she turns green, red and blue?
Will you still love me?"
"I'll always love you. Though you
will have to bath her."

"What if I forget to close the fridge
door and Baby Pog pulls everything out?
Will you still love me?"
"I'll always love you. Though there
won't be any food for tea."

"What if I pour Grandma Bear's lumpy porridge all over my head? Will you still love me?"
"I'll always love you. Though you will have to eat another bowlful. Now, why are you being such a silly bear this morning?"

For a few moments Alex didn't say anything.
Then he whispered, "What if I break your
favourite honey bowl? Will you still love me?"
"You know I'll always love you,"
said his mum. "Come on, Alex,
it must be time for breakfast."

And off they went to the kitchen.

"Oh no!" cried his mum
when she saw the pieces
of sticky china.
"That was my favourite
bowl, Alex."

"Sorry," said Alex. Two tears drizzled down his face. "You said you would still love me. I love *you*."

"Of course I love you,"
said Mother Bear,
hugging him.

"Hey, I've got an idea!" shouted
Alex, wriggling from her arms.
"What is it?" she asked.
"It's a surprise," Alex said
and he ran off to his bedroom.

He looked in his toybox . . .

He looked in his cupboard . . .

and he looked under his table.

At last Alex found what he wanted.

He got out his new paints, poured
some water into a jam jar and
swirled his paintbrush around.

A little while later, Alex came downstairs again.
"Look, it's a new bowl," he said. "See, it says 'Love
from Alex'. But be careful, the paint's still wet."
"I'll be *very* careful," said his mum, smiling.
"Because this is going to be my new
favourite honey bowl!"